Rise & Shine Mrs. Field!

Four Sisters

ISBN: 0692204202
ISBN-13: 978-0692204207

The barnyard is quiet.
The animals are asleep;
not a moo, not a neigh,
not a baa or a peep.
A loud "Cock-a-doodle-doo"
suddenly fills the air.
It awakens all the
animals
including the mare.

On that bright sunny
morning in early May,
it awakens Farmer Field to
start his busy day.
With a kiss on Mrs. Field's cheek
and a hug so tight,
he reminds his good wife,
he'll be gone until night.

"Please feed all the animals
their breakfast and lunch.
You remember my dear, they
are a hungry bunch."
"Certainly," she says with
a yawn and a sigh.
"But, a few more minutes of sleep,
my Sweetie Pie."

Now, the farm animals are
ready to start a new day
with their usual breakfast of
corn, oats and hay.
With their tummies growling,
the animals say, "Will anyone
feed us this morning in May?"
"Hey, rooster! Hey, rooster!"
moos the spotted black cow.
"It's your job to start the farm
day, please do it right now!"
So a trail of animals go to
Farmer Field's house,
and… tagging along goes a
little gray mouse.

Up flies the proud rooster
from the brown porch chair
and fills his lungs with
a big breath of air.
"Cock-a-doodle-doo,"
he loudly does crow.
"It is time for breakfast
so get up and go!"
But...

Mrs. Field only sleeps on,
snoring quite low.

Next the curly woolly sheep
begins to bleat.
"Wake up!" he says, "I want
something to eat!
Did you hear the rooster start
the day with his crow?
It's time to get up and feed us
you know!"
But…

Mrs. Field only smiles;
asleep on her pillow.

Then, up steps the really
hungry brown horse,
thinking she can wake
Mrs. Field, of course.
With a toss of her mane and
a very loud neigh,
"I would like some fresh
oats to begin my day!"
But…

Mrs. Field only dreams deeper,
not a word does she say.

“Step aside,” says the black
spotted cow,
“Let me wake her.
I certainly know how.”
Loudly, she moos next to
where Mrs. Field lay,
“Hay, lots of hay,
will make my day!”
But…

Mrs. Field rolls over;
in her bed she does stay.

Soon all the hens offer
an encouraging cluck
and challenge the geese
to try their luck.
With demanding
"Honk, honks"
and a flapping of wings,
the geese circle the bed
in a loud choral ring.
But…

Mrs. Field only snores on
and hears not a thing.

Into the room lumbered
the old gray mule
and bellowed quite loudly,
"Let's keep our cool.
It is certain Mrs. Field
has forgotten this bunch.
We can only hope
she'll awake in time for lunch."
But...

Mrs. Field rolled over and
gave her pillow a punch.

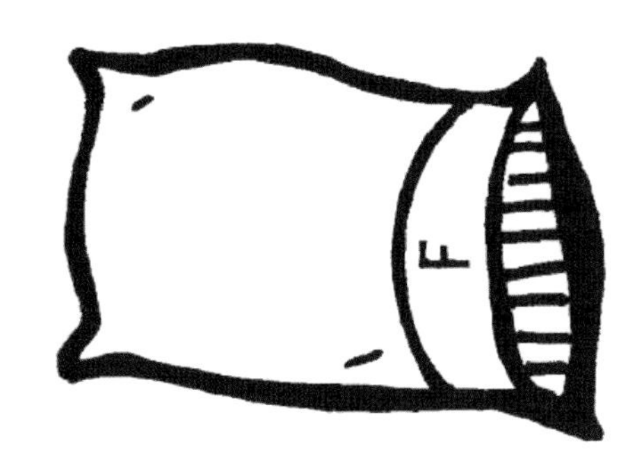

Then all the animals
begin to mope.
As they watch Mrs. Field
and sadly give up hope.
“We hear all our friends,
raising quite a fuss.
It seems obvious
no one will feed us!”
But...

Mrs. Field sleeps on
quite oblivious.

Then much to the barnyard
animals' surprise,
the small gray mouse says,
"Let me give it a try!"
He climbs right up
on the soft, wide bed
and creeps quite close
to Mrs. Field's head.

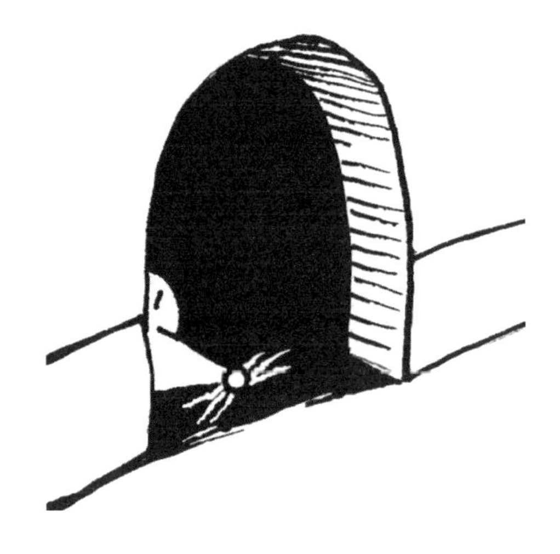

In her ear he softly speaks
three little words…

“Squeak, squeak, squeak.”

Then ever so slowly
Mrs. Field opens one eye,
she rolls over with a grunt
and a very soft sigh,
as all the farm animals
wait hopefully nearby.
“Oh, what a sweet dream!
Oh, what a good night!
I was sleeping so hard
with my eyes shut tight.”

HOME
SWEET
HOME

Then her eyes open wider,
she looks ‘round her bed,
and sees the farm animals
waiting to be fed.
“Why are you standing here
with so much work to do?”
Forgetting she’d been having
a really long snooze.
The hungry animals
start nodding
and give her big grins.
Thanks to the gray mouse,
Mrs. Field’s day finally begins.

"Hurray!" shout the animals,
"She's on her way!
We all will get fed
our corn, oats and hay!"
With a parade
of happy animals
taking the lead,
Mrs. Field
hustles to the barn
to get their feed.

But…

all morning the proud rooster
continues to crow;
as he is worrying
about what they all know.
Their stomachs will growl,
because lunch will come soon.

What if Mrs. Field
takes a nap
before noon?

THE FOUR SISTERS

Nancy Atkins, Martha Feild, Sue Petrick & Kakie Sawyer

Sean Murphy, Illustrator

Sean has been an elementary school art teacher for the past 23 years. He graduated from James Madison University with a B.F.A. with a printmaking concentration and has his Masters in Art Education from George Mason University. He resides in Fairfax, Va. with his wife and two children.

38125759R00021

Made in the USA
Lexington, KY
22 December 2014